Fancy NANCY

Butterfly Birthday

Written by
Jane O'Connor

Illustrated by
Robin Preiss Glasser

All you EVER needed to know about Butterflies!

The Big Book of Butterflies

HarperCollins *Children's Books*

For my favourite butterfly breeders—
Robby and Teddy—with love
—J. O'C.

For Edith Pick Lindner—for me, the
model of beauty and elegance
—R.P.G.

First published in hardback in the USA as Fancy Nancy: Bonjour, Butterfly by HarperCollins Publishers in 2008
This edition first published in paperback in Great Britian by HarperCollins Children's Books in 2009

HarperCollins Children's Books is a division of HarperCollins Publishers Ltd.

ISBN-13: 978-0-00-728877-9

HarperCollins Children's Books is a division of HarperCollins Publishers Ltd.

Text copyright © Jane O'Connor 2008
Illustrations copyright © Robin Preiss Glasser 2008

Typography by Jeanne L. Hogle

Visit our website at: www.harpercollins.co.uk

Printed and bound in China

Don't you think butterflies are exquisite?
(Exquisite is even fancier than beautiful.)

Whenever my friend Bree and I see one, we say, "Bonjour!" That's French for "hello!"

"Do butterflies understand French?" my dad asks.
"Maybe," I tell him.

Bree's birthday party is soon. Everything will look like butterflies – even the cake.

I show her how to turn the Bs into butterflies –  – on the invitations.

"You're so lucky your name begins with a B," I tell her.

Bree's
Butterfly
Birthday

Saturday
at noon

Come
as your
favourite
Butterfly

R.S.V.P.

R.S.V.P. is short for *Répondez s'il vous plaît*.

That's French for please reply.

I'm going as an azure butterfly.
My wings are bright blue and – what's that fancy
word for shiny? Oh, yes! Iridescent.

"Bree's party is this Saturday! I can't wait!" "Oh no!" cries my mum. "I totally forgot."

Then she says I can't go! My grandparents' anniversary party is the same day.

Mum says, "Bree's birthday is special. But being married for fifty years — that's exceptional. That's extraordinary!"

If my mother thinks using fancy words will make me feel better, she's wrong!

When I tell Bree I can't come, she is heartbroken.

For the next two days,
I scowl

and sulk

and storm around the house.

Mad is far too plain for how I feel.

I am furious!

On the train, the only person I talk to is
Marabelle. We mostly speak in French.

I perk up a little at the station.
My grandparents are so thrilled to see me.

Grandpa says, "It wouldn't be a party
without our glamorous granddaughter."

I must say, the City Squire Motel is quite elegant.
(That's a fancy word for fancy.) I curtsy to everyone.

There is a sweet machine in the hall
and an automatic ice dispenser.

In the bathroom are little
bottles of bath gel and shampoo
and cream.

Ooh la la! It's like being at a
beauty spa.

At the party, I have so much fun,
I forget to be furious.

Grandpa teaches me the cha-cha.

Waiters bring out tiny hot dogs
on silver platters.
"Mmm. Delicious,
darling," I tell my sister.
"You must try one."

Later I whisper, "I'm sorry
for the way I behaved. I am
ecstatic to be here."

It really is an extraordinary night.

The next morning, my mother wakes me up. "Grandma says the zoo here has a butterfly garden. Do you want to go?"

"Oui, oui, oui!" That's French for "yes, yes, yes!"

My grandparents meet us at the zoo. "Those are monarch butterflies on your tie," I tell Grandpa.

"My! You know a lot about butterflies," he says. "Yes," I admit. "I am practically an expert."

The butterfly garden is gorgeous.
(Gorgeous is also fancier than beautiful.)
I can't wait to tell Bree about it.

Suddenly a little blue butterfly flits toward me —
an azure butterfly.
All butterflies are special, but this one is extraordinary.
"Bonjour," I say.

You know what?

I am *nearly positive* butterflies understand French.